EXPLORE SOUTH AMERICA

by Veronica B. Wilkins

pogo

Ideas for Parents and Teachers

Pogo Books let children practice reading informational text while introducing them to nonfiction features such as headings, labels, sidebars, maps, and diagrams, as well as a table of contents, glossary, and index.

Carefully leveled text with a strong photo match offers early fluent readers the support they need to succeed.

Before Reading

- "Walk" through the book and point out the various nonfiction features. Ask the student what purpose each feature serves.
- Look at the glossary together. Read and discuss the words.

Read the Book

- Have the child read the book independently.
- Invite him or her to list questions that arise from reading.

After Reading

- Discuss the child's questions. Talk about how he or she might find answers to those questions.
- Prompt the child to think more. Ask: The Andes Mountains and Amazon River are notable landforms in South America. What landforms are near you?

Pogo Books are published by Jump!
5357 Penn Avenue South
Minneapolis, MN 55419
www.jumplibrary.com

Library of Congress Cataloging-in-Publication Data

Names: Wilkins, Veronica B., 1994- author.
Title: Explore South America / Veronica B. Wilkins.
Description: Minneapolis, MN: Jump!, Inc., 2020.
Series: A look at continents | Includes index.
Audience: Ages 7-10 | Audience: Grades 2-3
Identifiers: LCCN 2019030960 (print)
LCCN 2019030961 (ebook)
ISBN 9781645273004 (hardcover)
ISBN 9781645273011 (paperback)
ISBN 9781645273028 (ebook)
Subjects: LCSH: South America–Juvenile literature.
Classification: LCC F2208.5 .W54 2020 (print)
LCC F2208.5 (ebook) | DDC 980–dc23
LC record available at https://lccn.loc.gov/2019030960
LC ebook record available at https://lccn.loc.gov/2019030961

Editor: Susanne Bushman
Designer: Molly Ballanger

Photo Credits: Fedor Selivanov/Shutterstock, cover; hadynyah/iStock, 1, 5; Dirk Ercken/Shutterstock, 3; Seumas Christie-Johnston/Shutterstock, 4; Maciej Es/Shutterstock, 6-7 (foreground); Jaroslav74/Shutterstock, 6-7 (background); Saran Jantraurai/Shutterstock, 8-9; John Warburton Lee/SuperStock, 10-11; VarnaK/Shutterstock, 12-13; Ondrej Prosicky/Shutterstock, 14; Michel Nolan/robertharding/SuperStock, 15; Daniel Prudek/Shutterstock, 16-17; Aziz Ary Neto/Cultura Limited/SuperStock, 18; GUIZIOU Franck/Hemis/SuperStock, 19; imageBROKER/SuperStock, 20-21; OGphoto/iStock, 23.

Printed in the United States of America at Corporate Graphics in North Mankato, Minnesota.

TABLE OF CONTENTS

CHAPTER 1

THE ANDES AND THE AMAZON

Let's explore South America! Historians think Machu Picchu used to be a palace! These **ruins** are 7,710 feet (2,350 meters) up in the Andes Mountains.

Machu Picchu

The Andes Mountains are in western South America. They are about 5,500 miles (8,851 kilometers) long. High **plateaus** cover the northeast part of the **continent**.

Andes Mountains

South America is one of the seven continents. It is the fourth largest. It is almost totally surrounded by water.

The **equator** crosses through this continent. It is in both the Northern and Southern **Hemispheres**.

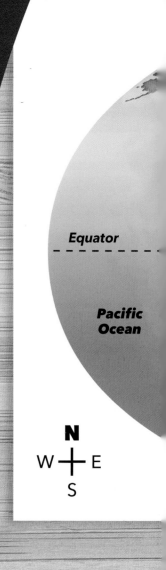

Equator

Pacific Ocean

N
W E
S

Arctic Ocean

NORTH AMERICA

EUROPE

ASIA

Atlantic Ocean

AFRICA

Pacific Ocean

Equator

SOUTH AMERICA

Equator

Indian Ocean

AUSTRALIA

Atlantic Ocean

Southern Ocean

ANTARCTICA

The Amazon Rain Forest covers much of the northern part of this continent. It is the largest **tropical** rain forest in the world. Millions of types of plants, animals, and insects live here. Monkeys swing from the many trees.

WHAT DO YOU THINK?

The Amazon Rain Forest is shrinking. Why? Humans are cutting down its trees. Some people want to protect this rain forest. Do you want to? Why or why not?

The Amazon River runs through the Amazon Rain Forest. It is the second longest river in the world! It is almost 4,000 miles (6,437 km) long.

Amazon
River

Patagonia

glacier

Plains are south of the Amazon Rain Forest. The far south of the continent is called Patagonia. This area is a plateau. Parts are **desert**. But there are **glaciers** here, too!

> ## DID YOU KNOW?
>
> Many islands surround the southern tip of South America. They are called Tierra del Fuego. Many travelers stop here on their way to Antarctica. Why? It is only around 620 miles (998 km) away.

CHAPTER 2
WILDLIFE AND CLIMATE

Around 3,000 kinds of birds live on this continent. Toucans fly in tropical forests. Flamingos live by lakes in the Andes Mountains. Penguins live on beaches in the far south!

◄····· toucan

Piranha hunt in rivers and lakes. Manatees swim in the Amazon River. They can weigh up to around 1,000 pounds (454 kilograms)!

manatee

The area of the Amazon Rain Forest is tropical. But the **climate** in the south is more **temperate**. Many peaks in the Andes Mountains are topped with snow. Llamas and alpacas live in these mountains.

TAKE A LOOK!

South America has many climate **regions**. Take a look!

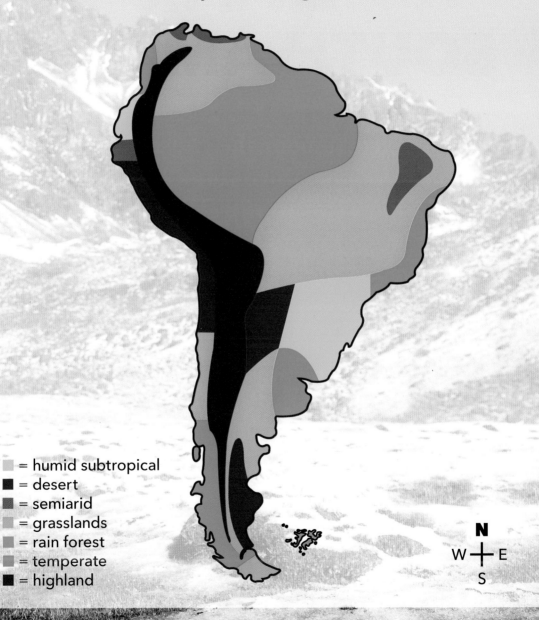

= humid subtropical
= desert
= semiarid
= grasslands
= rain forest
= temperate
= highland

N
W E
S

CHAPTER 3

LIFE IN SOUTH AMERICA

Most people live near the coast. Brazil has the most people. More than 200 million people live in this country! São Paulo is the city with the most people. It is on the Atlantic Coast.

São Paulo, Brazil

Bogotá, Colombia, is another large city. It is high in the mountains. Visitors can ride cable cars to a mountaintop church.

cable car

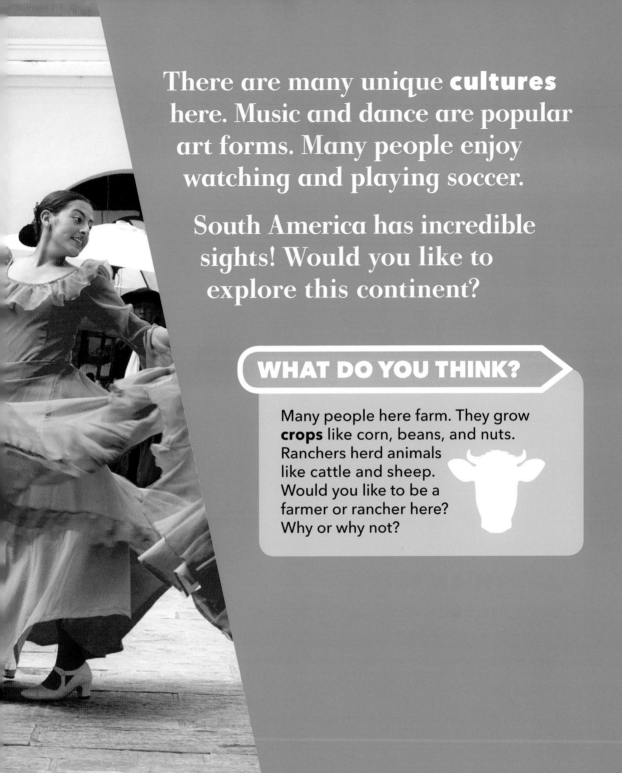

There are many unique **cultures** here. Music and dance are popular art forms. Many people enjoy watching and playing soccer.

South America has incredible sights! Would you like to explore this continent?

WHAT DO YOU THINK?

Many people here farm. They grow **crops** like corn, beans, and nuts. Ranchers herd animals like cattle and sheep. Would you like to be a farmer or rancher here? Why or why not?

QUICK FACTS & TOOLS

Andes Mountains

Amazon River

Amazon Rain Forest

Pacific Ocean

Atlantic Ocean

N
W + E
S

Patagonia

Tierra del Fuego

SOUTH AMERICA

Size: 6,878,000 square miles (17,813,938 square km)

Size Rank: Asia, Africa, North America, **South America**, Antarctica, Europe, Australia

Population Estimate: 430 million people (2019 estimate)

Exports: sugar, bananas, cocoa, cotton

Facts: South America makes up about 12 percent of Earth's land.

The Andes Mountains are the longest above-water mountain range in the world.

climate: The weather typical of a certain place over a long period of time.

continent: One of the seven large landmasses of Earth.

crops: Plants grown for food.

cultures: The ideas, customs, traditions, and ways of life of groups of people.

desert: A dry area where hardly any plants grow because there is so little rain.

equator: An imaginary line around the middle of Earth that is an equal distance from the North and South Poles.

glaciers: Very large, slow-moving masses of ice.

hemispheres: Halves of a round object, especially of Earth.

plains: Large, flat areas of land.

plateaus: Areas of level ground that are higher than the surrounding area.

regions: General areas or specific districts or territories.

ruins: The remains of something that has collapsed or been destroyed.

temperate: A climate that rarely has very high or very low temperatures.

tropical: Of or having to do with the hot, rainy areas of the tropics.

INDEX

TO LEARN MORE

Finding more information is as easy as 1, 2, 3.

1 Go to www.factsurfer.com

2 Enter "exploreSouthAmerica" into the search box.

3 Choose your book to see a list of websites.

FACT SURFER